P9-AOX-010

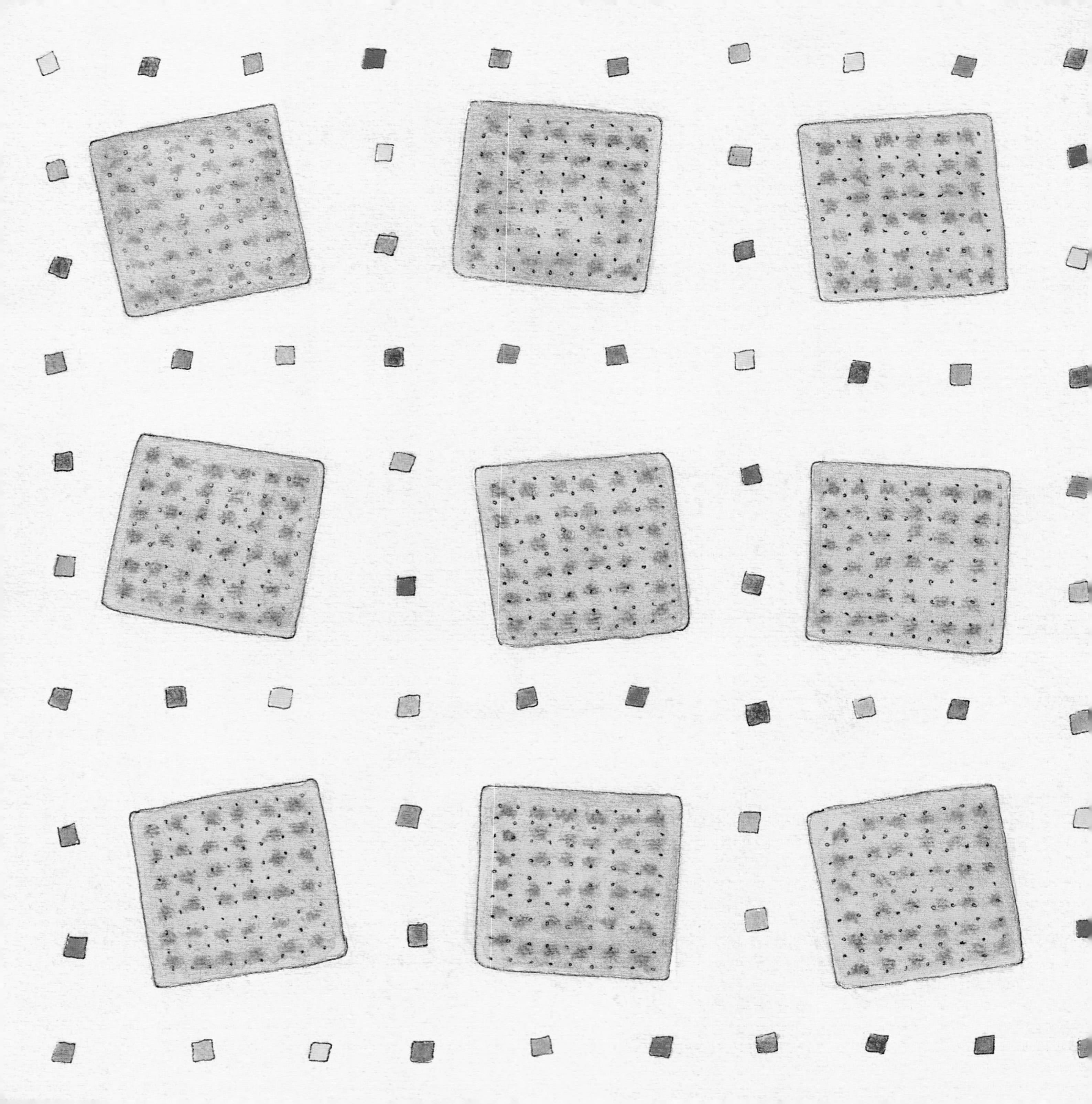

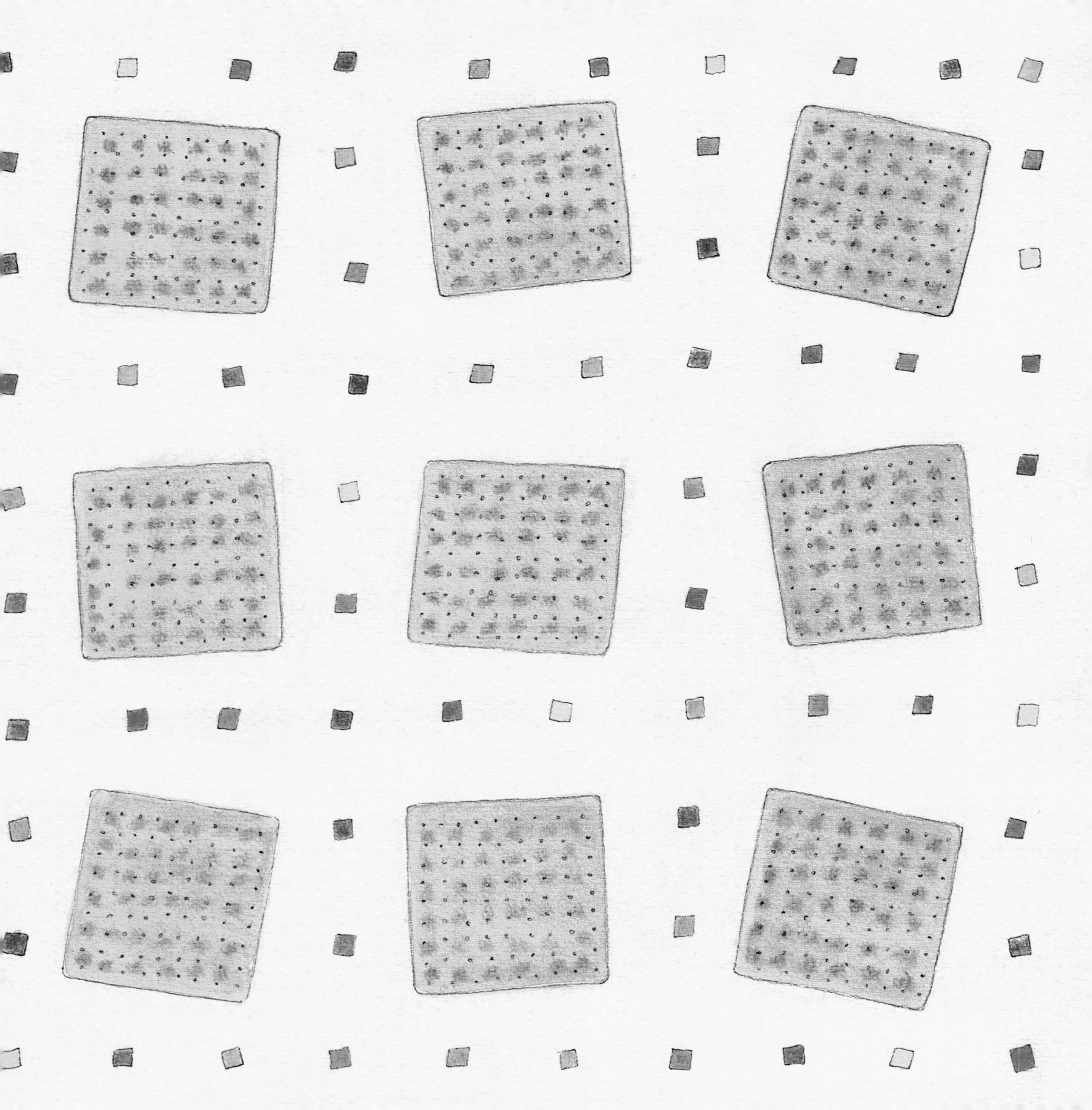

For Talia and Joseph – J.Z.
To Geoffrey and Audrey – J.B.C.

First edition for the United States, Canada, and the Philippines published 2003
by Barron's Educational Series, Inc.

First published in Great Britain in 2003 by
Frances Lincoln Limited, 4 Torriano Mews,
Torriano Avenue, London NW5 2RZ

All inquiries should be addressed to:
Barron's Educational Series, Inc.
250 Wireless Boulevard
Hauppauge, New York 11788
http://www.barronseduc.com

Library of Congress Catalog Card No. 2002107991
International Standard Book No. 0-7641-2267-3

Printed in Singapore
9 8 7 6 5 4 3 2

The Publishers would like to thank Bryan Reuben for checking the text and illustrations.

FESTIVAL TIME!

Four Special Questions

A Passover Story

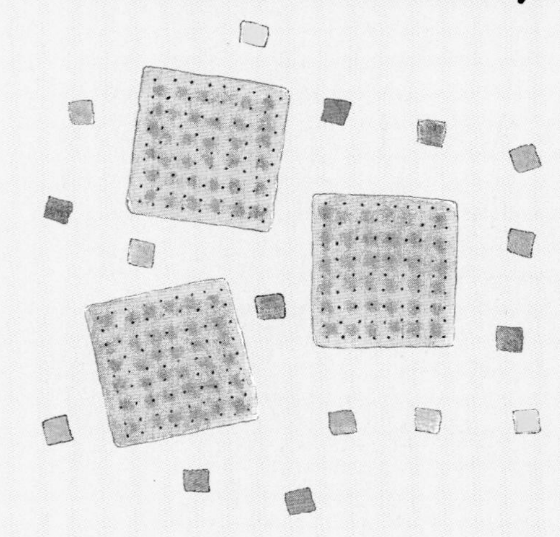

Jonny Zucker

Illustrated by Jan Barger Cohen

Passover is here and we remember how our people were once slaves in Egypt. I'm sweeping up all the bread crumbs with a feather.

For eight days we're going to eat matzoh, just like the Children of Israel did when they escaped from Egypt.

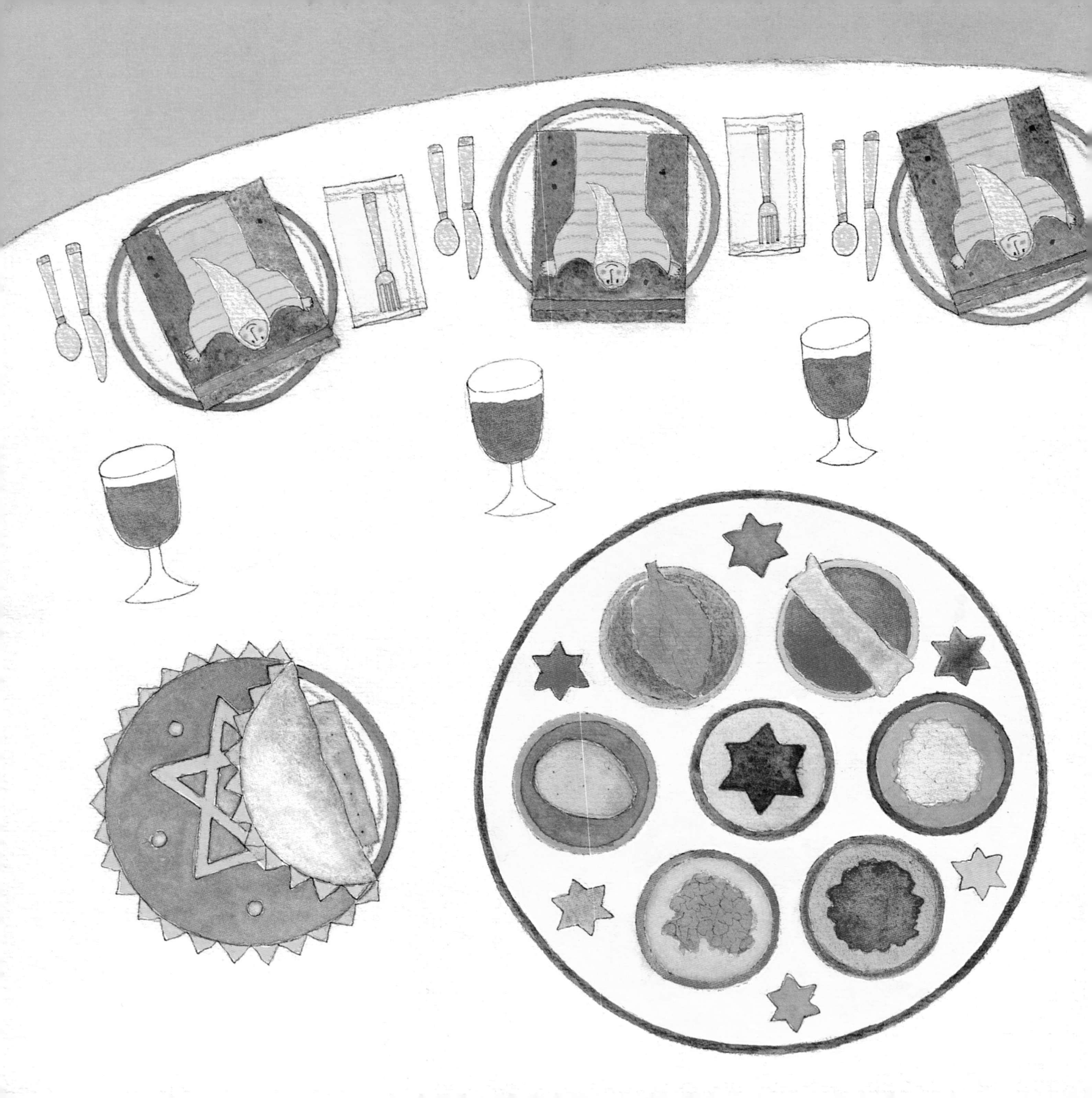

It's time for the Seder. I like to see the Seder plate with the six different types of food.

My brother asks four special questions about why this night is so different from other nights. I will be old enough to ask them next year.

We hear about ten plagues that God sent to the Egyptians.

River into Blood

Frogs

Boils

Hail

Lice
Insects
Death of Livestock
Locusts
Darkness
Death of the First Born

Dad hides the Afikoman—a special half piece of matzoh—and we all search for it. I find it first, but we all get a present!

We sing songs about the past
and the future to celebrate
our festival of freedom.

What is Passover about?

Many years ago, Pharaoh, the ruler of Egypt, made the Jews work as slaves. God told Moses to lead the Jews to the Promised Land. So Moses went to Pharaoh and said, "Let my people go!" But Pharaoh refused.

God, through Moses, brought ten plagues upon the Egyptians. After the tenth plague, the Jews finally fled from the land of Egypt under the cover of darkness. Before they fled, they had a quick meal of a paschal lamb and bread that didn't have time to rise. This unleavened bread is called **matzoh**. It is eaten today at Passover as a reminder of the escape from Egypt.

The night before Passover, the house is searched for **chametz**—bread in any form, even crumbs. When the chametz is found, it's thrown away or burned.

Passover is celebrated by having a **Seder**. Seder means "order." It is a time for everyone to hear the story and to talk about the time of slavery and the escape from Egypt. The story is told in a special order.

The story is retold in a special book called the **Haggadah**.

On the Seder table, three matzohs are placed on top of each other. The middle one is broken in half, and one-half (the **Afikoman**) is hidden. Later in the evening the children need to find the Afikoman, which means "dessert," so that the meal may be complete. The one who finds it gets a prize.

There is a special Seder plate. On this plate there is a bone shank, which symbolizes the paschal lamb eaten the night the Jews fled Egypt; an egg, which is a symbol of new life; **charoset**, a mixture of apples, nuts, and wine, to symbolize the mortar the Jewish slaves used for building; two forms of bitter herbs, which are a reminder of the bitter time the Jews had as slaves; and the **karpas** (a vegetable—normally parsley), which is dipped in salt water as a reminder of the tears the Jews shed.

During the Seder, the youngest child who is able asks four questions about why this night is different from all other nights. Four cups of wine are drunk during the evening, and a special cup is reserved for the prophet Elijah, who is supposed to bring peace.

Before and after the Seder meal, everyone sings songs, to bring joy to the evening and to remind us that once we were slaves, but now we are free.

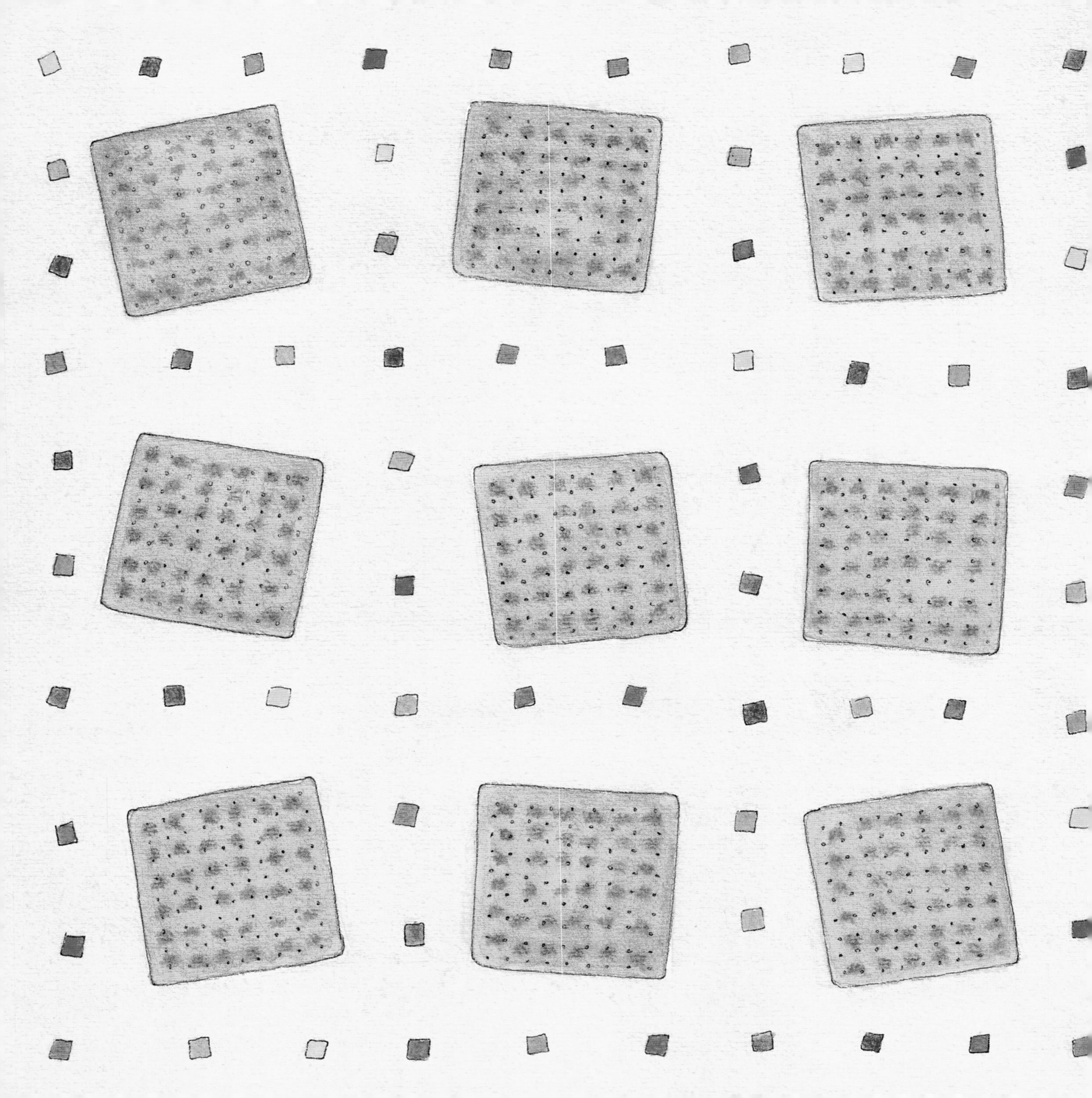

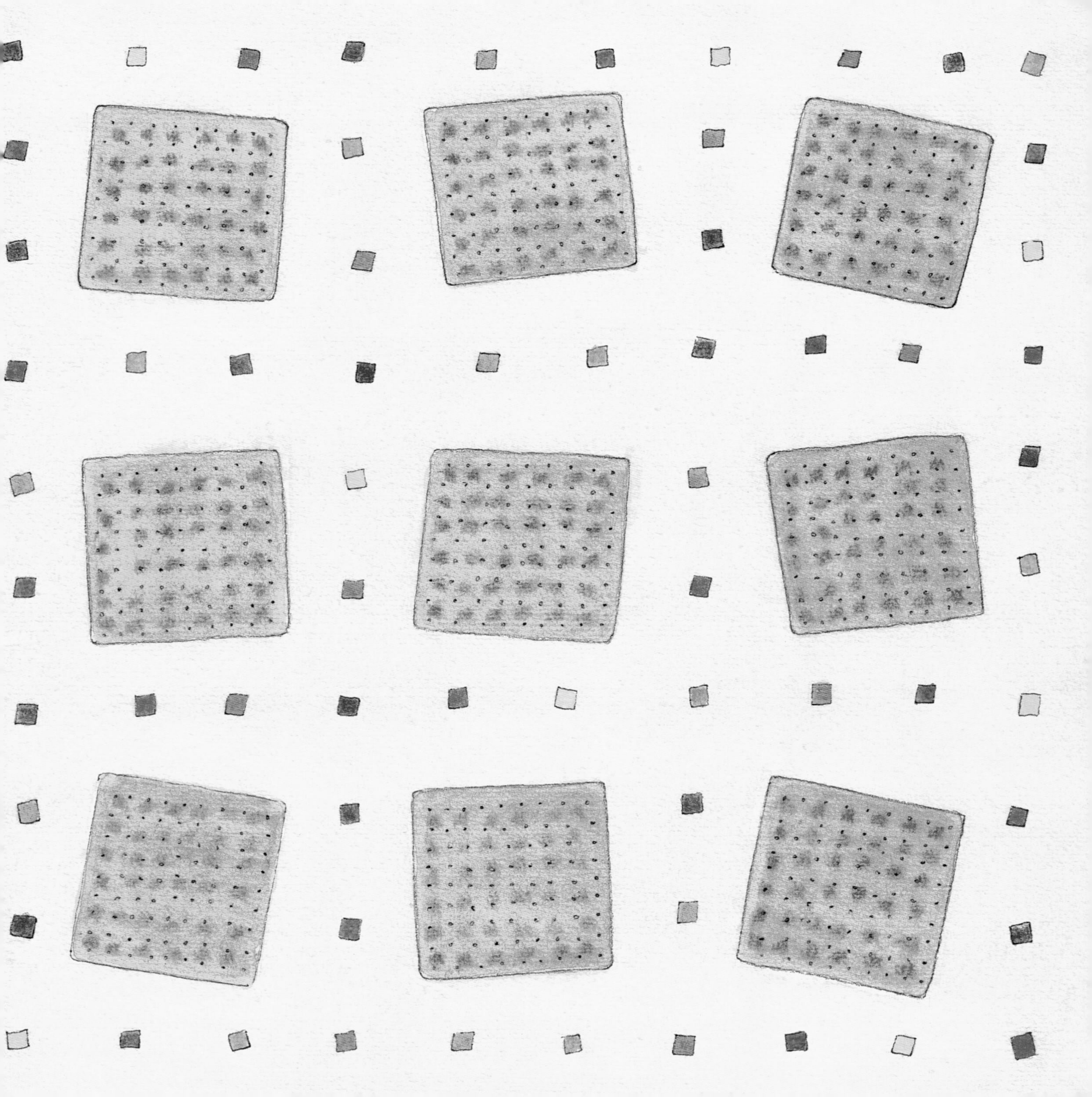